HOW TO DRAW
PEOPLE

Alastair Smith

Edited by Judy Tatchell

Designed by Nigel Reece

Illustrated by Graham Potts, Derek Brazell,
Kevin Lyles, Paddy Mounter, David Downton,
Nicky Dupays, Louise Nixon and Chris West

Photographs by Jane Munro Photography

Contents

Consultant: Richard Johnson

Drawing people

Drawing people is tricky because bodies are made up of so many different shapes. Still, if you follow the steps in this book you will find that you can get good results.

As well as helping you draw lifelike pictures, the book covers techniques such as cartooning and fashion illustration. This page contains some general tips.

● Get people to pose as models for you to draw. This enables you to check sizes and shapes of bodies while you draw them. If you cannot find a model, try copying a photo.

● Always plan a drawing by making a rough sketch, with pencil. This way you can ensure that the whole picture fits on your paper. Get the shapes right before you draw details.

● Draw big, rather than small. By doing this, you will be less likely to draw cramped-looking pictures. Also, you will find it easier to get detail into your pictures.

● Keep a rough book and pencil with you. Whenever you get a chance, make sketches in it. Keep old rough books, so that you can look back and see how your skills progress.

Materials

It is best to colour your pictures with the materials that you find easiest to use. However, you might like to try using a range of materials. This picture shows some of the effects that can be made with the materials that were used for the pictures in this book.

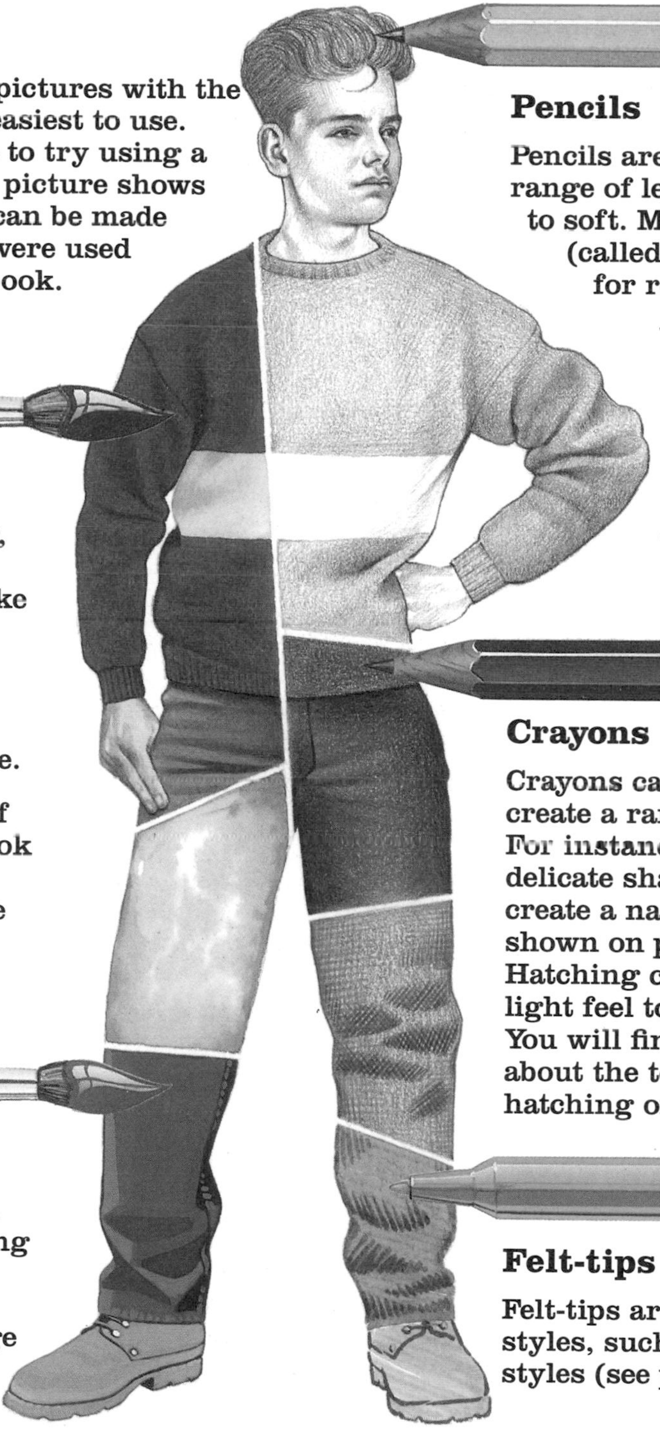

Watercolours

Mixed with a little water, watercolour paints can look strong and vivid, like this part of the boy's sweater. The picture on page 24 shows another example of this effect, drawn in a different style.

When mixed with a lot of water, the colours can look watery and soft. The picture at the top of page 13 shows a painting in this style.

Gouache

Gouache paints are vivid and are useful for creating flat areas. Poster paints give a similar effect and are cheaper, but the range of colours is narrower.

Pencils

Pencils are available with a range of leads, from hard to soft. Medium leads (called HB) are ideal for rough sketching.

You will see a rough pencil sketch on page 8. More detailed pencil drawings are on pages 30-31.

Crayons

Crayons can be used to create a range of effects. For instance, smooth, delicate shading helps to create a natural look, as shown on page 4. Hatching can give a loose, light feel to a picture. You will find more details about the technique of hatching on pages 10-11.

Felt-tips

Felt-tips are suited to unreal styles, such as comic strip styles (see page 21).

Heads and faces

Your face is the most expressive part of your body. Below the skin there are lots of tiny muscles, which you use all the time to make different expressions. These pages will help you to draw realistic-looking faces.

A face from the front

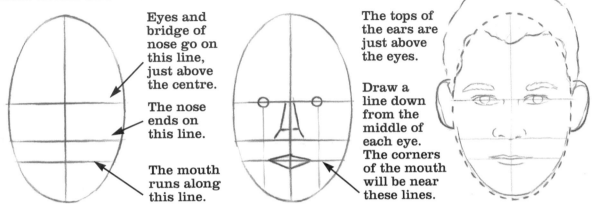

Eyes and bridge of nose go on this line, just above the centre.

The nose ends on this line.

The mouth runs along this line.

The tops of the ears are just above the eyes.

Draw a line down from the middle of each eye. The corners of the mouth will be near these lines.

Start by sketching an oval shape, with a pencil. Then draw construction lines on it, as shown above.

Using pencil, plot rough shapes around the lines. Use these shapes as guides to help you sketch features.

When you have drawn all the lines and shapes, start sketching features. Draw the hair as a single shape.

This picture is coloured with pencil crayons.

Swirls of dark colour are added to the hair.

Colour the face and hair with a layer of pale colour. Start to build shade with more of the same colour.

Instead of drawing hard lines around features, give them shape by adding shadow around them.

Use darker colours for areas in deep shadow. Add colour gradually until the face looks rounded.

Shading practice

It is quite difficult to make shading look convincing. For practice, draw and shade smooth, simple objects like those on the right. Look for light and shady parts before you begin.

Sketch the object in pencil first. Leave the white highlights blank, but colour the rest of the object with the lightest colour. Build up the shape by adding deeper shades of the same colour.

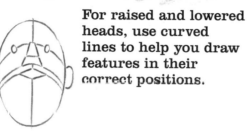

Heavier pressure was applied here to make the colour look darker.

Dark coloured crayons were used to colour the most shadowy parts.

Heads from different angles

The shapes here show you how to vary the construction lines in order to draw heads from different angles.

For raised and lowered heads, use curved lines to help you draw features in their correct positions.

A drawing from this angle is known as a three-quarter view.

A drawing from the side is called a profile.

Artist's tip

For practice, try drawing and shading features on their own, in close-up.

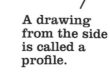

There is a selection of features for you to copy on pages 30-31.

5

Drawing bodies

What someone looks like depends just as much on their body proportions*, the way they stand and their clothes, as on their facial features.

When you draw whole figures, the first stage is to do rough sketches. Plot the body shapes and positions before you draw them in detail and colour them in. Below, you can see the way in which the people on the right were drawn. You could choose one of these people and copy the stages.

Rough sketches

Rough sketches should be done in pencil, using shapes like those on the right. Before you start, try to imagine the body parts below the clothing. This will help you to see how the clothes hang when you draw them.

Start your sketch by drawing the main body shapes shown in red, then the limb shapes shown in blue.

Don't stop to erase your mistakes. Just carry on sketching lightly until you think that the overall body shape looks correct. Then draw the clothes outline, shown in green.

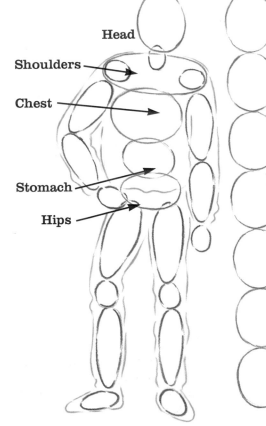

Head

Shoulders

Chest

Stomach

Hips

To check that the body parts in your sketch are in the right proportion, see how many head-sized ovals make up the overall height. If you are drawing an adult man, your subject will probably be about seven heads long.

Try doing rough sketches of some of the people at the top of this page. The more times you practise drawing body shapes like these, the easier they will become.

6   *When you are drawing a person, "proportion" means the size of one part of the body compared to another.*

Difficult angles

When a person is shown from a difficult angle, like the woman on the left, notice how some body shapes hide others. For instance, the head covers part of the shoulders, while the left arm hides the right arm.

Draw parts that are closer to you over the parts that they cover up. Rub out the parts that are covered.

Notice how the main body parts look as if they are squashed into each other.

How many heads?

People's proportions depend, for instance, upon what age they are and whether they are male or female. This guide shows some average proportions.

Women are about six and a half head-lengths.

People in their mid-teens are about six head-lengths.

Four year olds are about three and a half head-lengths.

Shading clothes

The folds, shadows and highlights formed on clothes can make them difficult to draw.

Most folds occur at joints like the knees and elbows. Shadows are formed where folds dip inwards (such as on the elbows of this coat). Highlights form where folds catch the light. Highlights and shadows are usually curved, because they form around the body.

When you draw clothes, sketch the clothes shapes over body shapes. Then sketch folds and creases lightly in pencil before applying any colour.

Leave the highlighted areas white, but apply a thin layer of colour over the rest of the garment.

Extra layers of colour, plus streaks of darker colour, help to show shadows and folds on the clothes.

Using models

Often, artists get someone to pose as a model for them when they draw. This helps because it gives the artist time to concentrate on the shapes a body makes in a particular position. Ask people you know to model for you, so that you can sketch them. It is extremely useful drawing practice.

Model positions

Position your models so that they are comfortable, or they will not be able to hold a pose for long. Try to make sure that they do not have to pose for more than 15 minutes at a time.

Start by drawing a rough sketch. Concentrate only on making the shapes and proportions look correct. Make your sketch look about as finished as the one shown here. Do not stop to erase mistakes.

As you make your sketch, notice how the parts of the body fit together. Include the hidden body shapes in the sketch, to help you draw the model in the correct proportions.

More poses

You could try sketching these poses, or you could get someone you know to model in positions like them. Chat to your model while you sketch, to keep them from getting bored.

Transforming a model

Some artists use their sketches of models as bases for other pictures, complete with different clothes and a new background. You could use images from magazines, films and books to give you ideas for how to transform your models.

Skydiver

The skydiver's clothes were copied from pictures in a book. His boot treads were copied from hiking boots.

To provide the basis for the drawing, the model lay on the floor with his feet close to the illustrator, as shown here.*

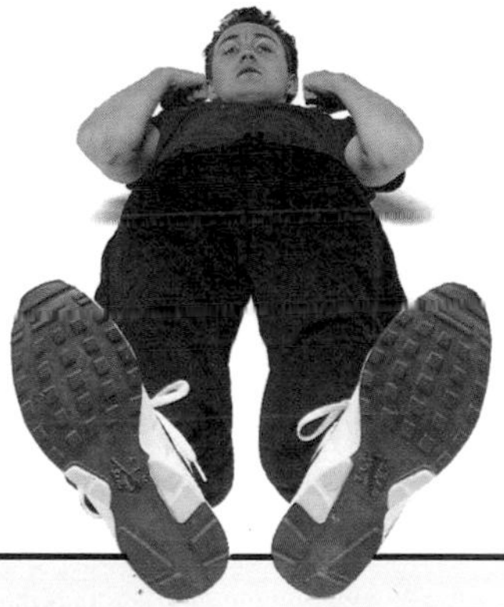

Light, hazy shading makes this parachute look far away.

To make the body look as if it is coming towards you, the shading becomes stronger as it gets closer to the feet.

Bright colours help this picture to look exciting.

Shading practice

For extra shading practice, try drawing your models as if their bodies are a collection of smooth metal tubes and containers.

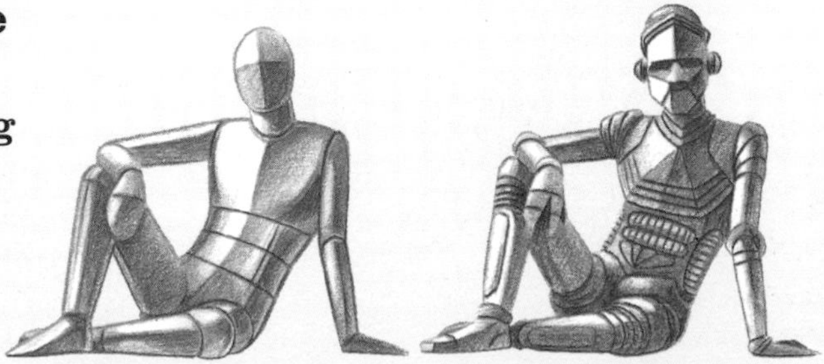

As a finishing touch you could add buttons, knobs, tubes and flashing lights, to turn your sketched figure into an android.

*The angle of this picture makes the body look distorted. Find out more about drawing figures like this on pages 14-15.

Portraits

Portraits are detailed pictures of people. They are usually, but not always, fairly realistic and they may help to show the subject's personality.

Draw a portrait when your subject is relaxed and will sit still for a long time, for example, while he or she is reading, or watching television.

Starting the portrait

First, draw the rough head shape. Then sketch the body shapes in proportion to the size of the head. (See the panel on the right.)

To help you position the body parts correctly in relation to each other, check which parts line up with one another.

In this drawing the subject's right eye, right shoulder and right knee all line up. The right shoulder, left knee and left ankle also line up. In your portraits, sketch faint lines to help you keep the body parts lined up.

This portrait is shaded with crayons, using a technique called hatching. See the **Artist's tip** on the opposite page, for more about hatching.

Faint lines like these help to line up the body parts.

Checking proportions

To help work out the proportions, first look at the head, with one eye shut. Then measure it with a pencil held at arm's length, as shown.

Line up your thumb with the chin.

Use this measurement to see how many head-lengths make up the rest of the body.

Your portrait can be as big or small as you like. However, keep the number of head-lengths in the body the same in your portrait as in life.

Backgrounds

Use background colours that contrast with your subject, like the plain colours shown here. This will help people to focus on the subject of the portrait.

To help show your subject's personality, you could draw them with some of their favourite possessions.

Artist's tip

Hatching is a technique well-suited to shading with pencils, crayons or pens.

Make lots of short, diagonal strokes. For faint shading, press down lightly. Space the hatches quite far apart.

Where shading is stronger, do hatches closer together. Press down quite hard to make the colours strong.

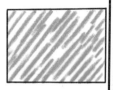

Where shading is strongest, try cross-hatching. Draw the hatches in a criss-cross pattern close together.

Cameos

Cameos are silhouettes of heads drawn in profile, with crisp, accurate outlines. They look most effective if you make them small, like the one below.

First, sketch a head shape in pencil. Then plot the shape of the face and the hair.

Make the outline very clean and detailed. Keep checking against your subject.

For the finished effect, cut out an oval shape around the silhouette.

Special effects

Artists often arrange lights to help them create special effects with real models. These pages will show you how to create some special effects of your own. For best results, use angle-poise lamps or a bright flashlight.

Horror show

To make your model look like a terrifying character from a horror movie, shine a single light up from the floor, just in front of them.

Put the light on the floor, as shown in this photograph.

The light should be bright, to make shadows as sharp as possible.

Using watercolour

Apply watercolours in layers, called washes, starting with the lightest colour. Unless the previous wash is dry before you paint over it, the colours will blend. To create shadowy areas, add streaks of darker colour over a still-damp wash.

Grisly details

Add details, like a trickle of blood from the mouth and bloodshot eyes, to make the character complete.

For the background, use cold colours (see pages 18-19), like blues and greys, to give the scene a moonlit quality.

Artist's tip

Use gouache or poster paints when you paint details over watercolours (like the trickle of blood in this picture). These paints keep their true colours when used over watercolours.

True Romantic

For a romantic lighting effect, use two lights, as positioned in the photo below.

A light shone from behind the subject is called a backlight.

Position the backlight so that it gives a soft halo around the subject. The front light should be less bright. Use it to cut down the shadows on the face.

If you want to draw a particular mood, ask your model to imagine the mood and show it on their face. This subject looks sad, as if she is remembering a lost love.

Make your watercolours look soft, as in this picture, by mixing your paints with lots of water. If your mixture is too dark, the picture will look gloomy.

Mystery

To make a person look mysterious, like a prowling spy or private eye, shine a single light on them, from the side.

A light shone from the side is called a sidelight.

Clothes can help to set an atmosphere in a picture. Here, the subject is shown in a coat with a turned-up collar, to help him look suspicious.

Paint in black and white, with touches of light grey. To make shadows very dark, mix your black paint with hardly any water.

To look threatening, the model tilted his head and frowned.

Dramatic pictures

A picture can look dramatic if it captures movement, like the drawing on the right. Another way to make a picture look dramatic is to draw it from an unusual angle, like the one at the bottom of the opposite page.

The skateboarder's left arm is also foreshortened.

Altering proportions

The picture on the right shows an example of how the proportions of body parts can look distorted when they are drawn from a certain angle. Because the front arm is stretched towards you, the right hand looks big in proportion to the rest of the body and the arm looks squashed. This effect is called foreshortening.

This picture shows off the skateboarder's balance and poise.

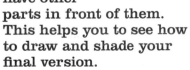

To begin, sketch rough shapes. Start from the closest-looking part. Notice that closer parts cover up parts that are further away.

Rub out parts which have other parts in front of them. This helps you to see how to draw and shade your final version.

Foreshortening

As an example of foreshortening, notice how, as this person's arm raises, it seems to get shorter.

The distance between the raised hand and the body looks squashed. The hand looks large, as it is closer to you than before.

Drawing foreshortened figures is tricky. Practise the technique by sketching rough shapes only.

Action pictures

A picture of an exciting event looks really effective if you show it at the most action-packed moment, or even a split-second before, to add a feeling of suspense. Below are some action pictures drawn from dramatic angles.

Practice tip

Practise foreshortening by sketching long objects from various angles.

For further practice you could try drawing parts of yourself, like an arm, leg or hand.

Adding details

When you draw a dramatic picture, try to include details which will add atmosphere and excitement to the event. The labels show how drama can be added to a picture.

Body positions. Here, the leg positions suggest that the man is swinging from the ledge.

Facial expressions. Here, the face shows the person's grim determination to hang on to the wall.

Background. Here it shows a terrifying situation from a very dramatic angle.

People in perspective

Perspective drawings are based on the fact that the further away things are, the smaller they look. Things in the background are made to look as if they are the right size and in the correct position, compared with things in the foreground. On the opposite page, notice how the railway track, trees and people all look smaller as they get further away. The railway track disappears at a point (called the vanishing point) in the middle of the picture. Nothing is visible beyond the vanishing point.

Sketching a scene

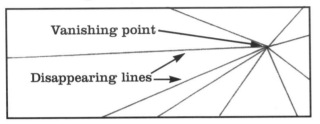

Start by drawing the vanishing point. Next, sketch guide lines (called disappearing lines) from the vanishing point. They will help you to draw distant things in proportion to things that are close up.

Sketch the main features of the scene, using the disappearing lines as guides. In the picture on the right the buildings, railway track and trees have all been sketched in this way. See below for tips about drawing people in the scene.

People in a line

When showing people in a line, directly behind each other, sketch the closest person first.

Draw disappearing lines from the person's feet and head. Show the people behind inside these lines.

People not in a line

For people not directly behind one another, sketch an upright line inside the disappearing lines, level with

where you want another person to go. Draw horizontal lines across from this, where the lines meet.

16

Creating depth

This scene was drawn in a comic style. (There are more details about comic styles on pages 20-21.) The unfinished parts of this scene should help to show how it was constructed. The tips dotted around the picture show several ways in which you can give an impression of distance in a scene.

In a realistic picture, colours get paler towards the horizon. Comic colouring is usually simpler, though, so the same colours are used in the foreground and background in this picture.

Repeated objects reinforce the sense of perspective.

Draw repeated objects closer together as they go into the distance.

People and objects in the foreground are drawn in more detail than in the background.

Put some figures partly in front of others. This connects the figures and leads your eye into the picture.

Using colour

The colours you use will affect the mood of a picture. You can make the mood more obvious by drawing and colouring in a particular style.

Baggy suit

The trumpet player is wearing a 1940s baggy suit. The colours suggest the atmosphere of a dimly lit jazz club. The drawing style emphasizes the size and bagginess of the suit.

Felt-tips were used to create strong, simple blocks of colour. These blocks give the picture a bold feel.

Notice how all the shapes look angular, especially at the shoulders, elbows and knees.

Drawing the figure

Sketch the rough body shapes first, in pencil.

Draw the clothes and their folds with mostly straight lines, around the body shapes.

Use the fold lines as guides to divide your drawing into areas of different shades.

Cold and warm colours

Colours are sometimes described as cold or warm. This is because people associate certain colours, such as blues and greys, with cold things, such as steel or the sea. They associate oranges, yellows and reds with warm things, such as fire and the Sun.

Cold colours

High speed skier

The skier's clothes are coloured with streaks of crayon, to make it look as if she is travelling very fast. Most of the clothes' colours are bright and warm. When used on this subject, they help convey a feeling of danger and excitement.

Building the colour

Begin by shading the lines quite far apart, as shown here. Leave highlight areas with hardly any lines.

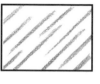

Build up colour in darker areas by drawing the lines closer together.

Add darker shades over light shades to create shadows. The light and dark areas will make the body look solid.

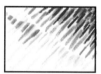

The warm coloured clothes stand out against the cool coloured background. If you want a background colour to contrast with the subject, colour the subject first and then choose a suitable, contrasting colour for the background.

Warm colours

In pictures, colours help to create atmospheres linked with coldness or warmth. For example, the blues in the picture on the previous page make it look sharp and cool. The woman's coat shown on page 6 is coloured in a warm colour to make it look cosy.

19

Comic strip people

Comic strips first appeared about a hundred years ago, in newspapers. Since then, several different styles of comic drawing have become popular. On these pages are examples of two of the most popular styles.

◀ Tintin, a daring young crimefighter, with his dog Snowy. Tintin's clothes are drawn in detail but his head is not. His simple facial features make him look honest and friendly.

"Funnies" style

The style of characters like those on the right was first used in newspapers in the USA, where comic strips in newspapers are called "funnies". The characters usually look silly to match the crazy adventures that they have.

The figures on the right show typical "funnies" features. You could use these examples to inspire you when you draw characters of your own.

Asterix the Gaul's headgear ▶ and dagger show that he is a warrior. However, his huge, rounded features and cheerful face make him look funny not threatening.

◀ Minnie the Minx, a mischievous character from the British comic *The Beano*. Her mouth, knobbly knees and wild expressions emphasize her cheeky sense of humour.

Comic drawing stages

Whatever comic drawing style you use, follow these steps when you create a character. Take time to work out the shape and expression of your character, so that it looks as interesting as possible.

To develop ideas for a character's look and personality, do a series of doodles.

Next, choose the position for your character, then make a sketch of it in pencil.

Superhero style

The first superhero-style comic character was Flash Gordon. He was first drawn in the 1930s. The superheroes shown here were created for Marvel comics in the 1960s.

Superheroes

Superheroes are very fit and muscular and they have abilities that ordinary humans cannot match. Their heights are about nine head-lengths, which exaggerates the power of their bodies. Their faces are usually handsome.

Some superheroes hide their true identities beneath masks. Most wear a tight-fitting costume when they perform their heroics.

You could try your own versions of the poses shown here. Design your own costumes for the superheroes to wear.

Spider-Man. His special powers enable him to climb up anything and spin enormous webs. Often, he uses his webs to trap criminals.

Sue Richards, member of a crime-fighting group called the Fantastic Four. She has the power to disappear, so she is also known as the Invisible Girl. Notice how her colour fades as she becomes invisible.

Complete the sketch by adding details like facial features, expressions and clothes.

Go over your pencil lines with a fine ink pen. Then rub out any pencil lines.

Colour the clothes with strong, bright colours. Felt-tips are ideal.

Caricatures

Caricatures deliberately overstate a person's features to make them look funny. The best ones also manage to highlight the subject's personality. These pages will show you how to make your own caricatures.

Before you start drawing, imagine the person that you want to caricature. Remember which features make the strongest impression in your mind. Make those features the most obvious ones in your caricature.

Building a caricature

Features like glasses, bushy hair, braces, big boots and a confident stance make this subject ideal for a caricature.

Start by tracing or copying an original photo or life-like illustration. Show the important features of the original picture. Simplify the picture by using as few lines as possible. Do not show any shading.

When you have done your simplified drawing, decide how you want to alter your subject. Then trace your simplified drawing, making changes to the sizes and shapes of features to change the person's look.

Enlarge some features and shrink others. To enlarge a feature, trace slightly outside the lines of the previous drawing (for example, see the head and glasses above). To shrink a feature, trace inside it.

Celebrities

Famous people (like these movie stars) make good subjects for caricatures. Their larger-than-life personalities should give you a clue to how to exaggerate their features.

Oliver Hardy

Marilyn Monroe

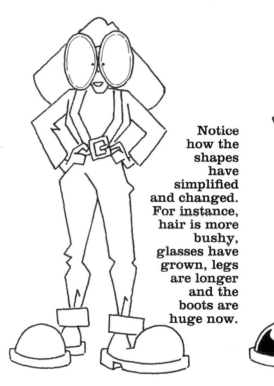

Notice how the shapes have simplified and changed. For instance, hair is more bushy, glasses have grown, legs are longer and the boots are huge now.

Keep doing new tracings, altering the features at every stage, until you think that your caricature is extreme enough. After several stages of tracing, the drawing should have altered drastically.

Make sure that the original subject can be recognized in the final drawing. Ink and colour the caricature in the same way as a comic character. (See pages 20-21 for how to do this.)

New adventures

You could show caricatures in crazy, comic-style situations and adventures.

Sketch the rough body positions, then draw the caricature's features and clothes over the shapes.

23

Fashion illustration

Fashion illustrators draw people in styles which make clothes look as glamorous as possible. They usually base their illustrations on elegant figures that are at least eight heads long.

Sketching the pose

First, sketch a posing model. You could base your sketch on a photo from a fashion magazine. Show the proportions of a real person.

To make the drawing look more thin and elegant, sketch versions with lengthened body parts, especially the arms and legs.

Draw the outlines of clothes over the body sketch. Simplify the clothes shapes, to give your picture a sleek appearance.

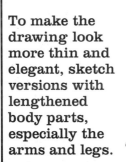

Colouring the sketch

To paint a picture in watercolours, like the one on the left, follow these steps:

1. First, colour the skin tones and hair colour. Mix your paint with a lot of water, to make the colours look watery. Colour shapes like the knees with slightly darker tones, using a minimum of detail.

2. To colour the clothes, mix the paint with only a little water. Paint with bold brushstrokes and do not try to show close detail. Exaggerate highlights by leaving large areas of white (as on the left leg). Paint simplified shadows on top of the clothes colour.

3. When the clothes and skin colours have dried, give dark outlines to the picture. Try to paint these lines with single brushstrokes. This will make the body shape look fluid and curved. Also, add dark lines to the hair to give it texture.

4. Draw the details (like facial features and ear-rings) last, when the paint is dry. Sketch them in pencil and then draw over them with a fine ink pen.

Collage

In a collage, portions of coloured paper are cut out and stuck down instead of using paints. For a stylized effect, the shapes should be cut with jagged edges.

Building the collage

Sketch the pose and then lengthen the body shapes, as you would do for a fashion illustration. Add clothes shapes to the sketch.

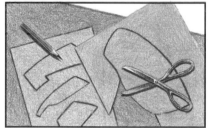

Trace the final sketch on to coloured paper. Cut out the tracings, making your cuts as straight as possible.

Glue the cut-out pieces of paper on a fresh piece of paper or card. Then follow the tips on the right to create a finished collage.

As an alternative, you could use a felt-tip pen to emphasize the shapes.

Stick smaller bits of coloured paper on to the larger pieces for details, like the stripes on this soccer kit.

Sketch the body and facial features over the stuck down paper, using simple, flowing lines to create the shapes.

Paint over the sketched lines with black watercolour, mixed with a little water. Use a thin brush and paint with light, fast sweeps of the brush.*

You can paint a variety of thick and thin lines, depending on how hard you press on the brush.

A colour patch behind the figure suggests the background.

Painted features do not have to follow the paper shapes.

Egyptian-style art

It can be amusing to use an art style that is inappropriate to your subject matter. For instance, the picture opposite shows a visit to a modern dentist, done in the style of an Ancient Egyptian painting.

This page points out some features of the Ancient Egyptian style, which was used about 3,000 years ago.

Style guide

Ancient Egyptian art does not show any perspective. People in the background are painted higher up the page but the same size as people in the foreground.

Figures never show any foreshortening. Things are shown either from the front or the side. When people are shown, their shoulders face outwards while their faces, stomachs and legs are shown from the sides.

Ancient Egyptians usually drew their pictures on stone walls, or on pieces of paper (called papyrus) made from strips of reed. To show a similar texture to these, draw your scene on rough brown paper or ordinary brown wrapping paper.

Important people are painted larger than ordinary people.

Often, large animals are shown smaller than humans, to symbolize that humans were thought to be more important than animals.

Usually, people are made to look skinny and long in proportion to their heads.

Notice how the hair and face are simplified. Faces do not show any feelings.

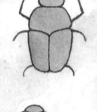

Hieroglyphics

The simplified objects above are examples of hieroglyphics, a written code made up of symbols and pictures. Ancient Egyptian artists used them to help explain their pictures to the viewer.

A trip to the dentist

Use watercolours to colour a picture in this style. For the clothes, paint in flat washes, using earthy, natural looking shades in keeping with the colours in an Ancient Egyptian picture.

You could paint a textured background on white paper, using very watery washes. To create a smudged effect, paint each new wash while the previous one is still damp.

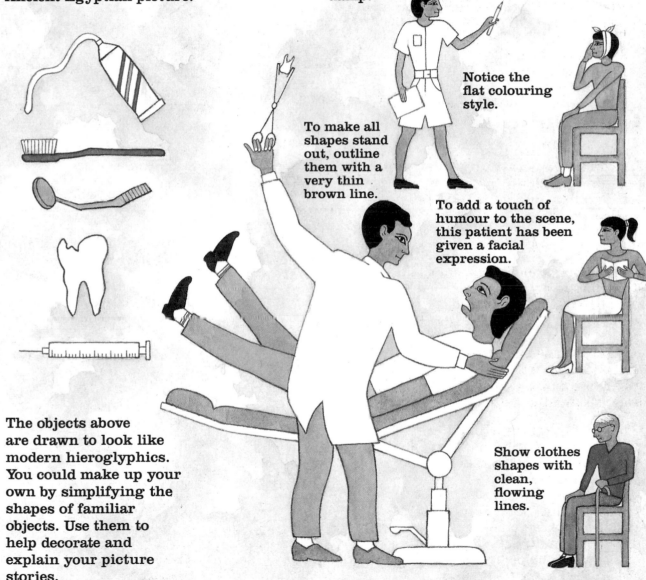

Notice the flat colouring style.

To make all shapes stand out, outline them with a very thin brown line.

To add a touch of humour to the scene, this patient has been given a facial expression.

The objects above are drawn to look like modern hieroglyphics. You could make up your own by simplifying the shapes of familiar objects. Use them to help decorate and explain your picture stories.

Show clothes shapes with clean, flowing lines.

Making masks

If you like drawing people, you will probably enjoy making masks. A mask hardly ever looks like a real face, but it highlights and exaggerates certain elements of a face to ensure that it has lots of character.

Masks are not difficult to make. All you need is some thin, flexible card, some elastic, scissors and a pencil and crayons, felt-tips or pens.

Mask-making steps

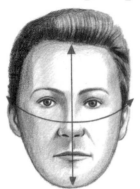

Start by measuring the face of the person who will wear the mask.

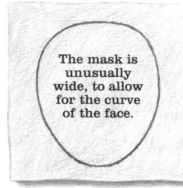

The mask is unusually wide, to allow for the curve of the face.

Draw the face shape on your card, according to your measurements.

Draw hair over and around the original design shape.

Do not draw face shadows on your mask. Real shadows will form on it when it is worn.

Plot the features in pencil. Colour the mask, then cut it out.

Holding the mask on

Reinforce the holes with adhesive tape.

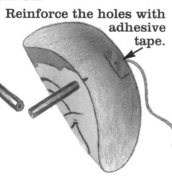

Mark the positions for two holes, about 1cm (almost ½in) in from the widest points on either side of the mask.

Use the point of a pencil to make holes in the mask. Push elastic into the holes and tie it in place with knots.

Making eye holes

Work out where eye holes should go. Carefully, mark the positions for the eye holes with a pencil.

Pierce tiny eye holes in the mask. The holes do not have to be in the same place as the eyes of the mask design.

Mask styles

Masks can be just for fun but in some parts of the world people wear them for superstitious reasons or during religious ceremonies or festivals, such as carnivals.

The actors in some traditional forms of drama wear masks which show the identities of the characters. Here are some ideas that you could copy or adapt.

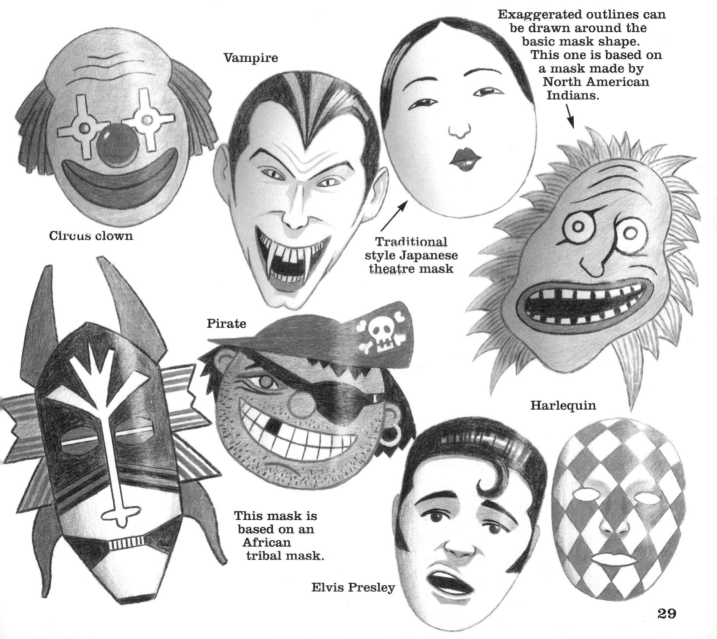

Vampire

Exaggerated outlines can be drawn around the basic mask shape. This one is based on a mask made by North American Indians.

Circus clown

Traditional style Japanese theatre mask

Pirate

Harlequin

This mask is based on an African tribal mask.

Elvis Presley

Body parts to copy

Many people spoil a well-proportioned picture by making mistakes when they draw the features in detail. To avoid this problem, practise drawing close-ups of features as often as you can, copying them from life or from photos.

You could copy the body parts on these pages for practice. Do not colour them in – concentrate on drawing the shapes, highlights and shadows. You could even use these shapes in your own pictures.

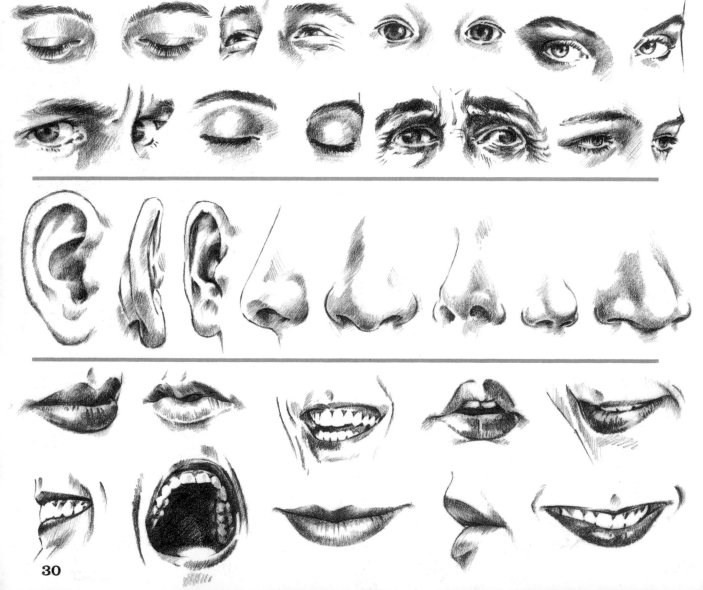